The Journey Home from Grandpa's

Written by Jemima Lumley

Illustrated by Sophie Fatus

Sung by Fred Penner

Barefoot Books
step inside a story

The yellow car drives down
the bouncy, bumpy road,
The bouncy, bumpy road,
the bouncy, bumpy road,

The yellow car drives down
the bouncy, bumpy road,
On the journey home from Grandpa's.

The white helicopter whizzes
up and down and round,
Up and down and round,
up and down and round,

The white helicopter whizzes
up and down and round,
On the journey home from Grandpa's.

The purple train speeds along
the shiny railway track,
The shiny railway track,
the shiny railway track,

The purple train speeds along
the shiny railway track,
On the journey home from Grandpa's.

The pink tractor bumps across
the brown and muddy field,
The brown and muddy field,
the brown and muddy field,

The pink tractor bumps across
the brown and muddy field,
On the journey home from Grandpa's.

The green digger scoops up
the icky sticky sand,
The icky sticky sand,
the icky sticky sand,

The green digger scoops up
the icky sticky sand,

On the journey home from Grandpa's.

The black crane lifts up
the heavy pile of bricks,
The heavy pile of bricks,
the heavy pile of bricks,

The black crane lifts up
the heavy pile of bricks,
On the journey home from Grandpa's.

The blue barge floats along
the cool and still canal,
The cool and still canal,
the cool and still canal,

The blue barge floats along
the cool and still canal,
On the journey home from Grandpa's.

T O Y S

The orange truck hurries to
the toyshop in the town,
The toyshop in the town,
the toyshop in the town,

The orange truck hurries to
the toyshop in the town,
On the journey home from Grandpa's.

The red fire engine rushes
very quickly past,
Very quickly past,
very quickly past,

The red fire engine rushes
very quickly past,
On the journey home from Grandpa's.

The yellow car stops at
    the front door of my house,
The front door of my house,
    the front door of my house,

The yellow car stops at
the front door of my house,

We've come home again from Grandpa's.

Grandpa's House

white helicopter

purple train

yellow ca[r]

red fire engine

Our House

To my fab children
Ruby and Vincent,
with all my love — J. L.

For my father and mum,
who drove me on the
artistic way — S. F.

Barefoot Books
294 Banbury Road
Oxford, OX2 7ED

Barefoot Books
2067 Massachusetts Ave
Cambridge, MA 02140

First published in Great Britain by Barefoot Books, Ltd
and in the United States of America by Barefoot Books, Inc in 2006
This paperback edition first published in 2011
All rights reserved

Lead vocals by Fred Penner. Musical composition,
arrangement and lead vocals © 2006 by Fred Penner
Animation by Karrot Animation, London

Graphic design by Louise Millar, London
Reproduction by Grafiscan, Verona, Italy
Printed in China on 100% acid-free paper by Printplus, Ltd
This book was typeset in Family Dog
The illustrations were prepared in acrylics

ISBN 978-1-84686-658-6

British Cataloguing-in-Publication Data:
a catalogue record for this book is available from the British Library

Library of Congress Cataloging-in-Publication Data is available under
LCCN 2005030372

5 7 9 8 6 4